T0365789

KIRTI'S FUTURE

ISBN: Softcover   978-1-5434-1075-4
        EBook   978-1-5434-1076-1

Print information available on the last page

Rev. date: 03/24/2017

To order additional copies of this book, contact:
Xlibris
1-888-795-4274
www.Xlibris.com
Orders@Xlibris.com

KIRTI'S FUTURE

MARSHA FRANKS

Illustrated by: Elenei Rae Pulido

Kirti Adetta and her family live in West Bengal, India. She lives with her father, Marrish Adetta, her mother, Ria, her two brothers, Denny and Davis, and her cousin, Raj. Kirti's father is a share cropper for a huge land owner. There are large open fields around her house on all sides except for one where there are large rocks. Her father works in the fields that grow wheat, barley and maize. These are the crops that her family shares with the land owner. They get a portion of the income from the crops which is barely enough for them to buy enough food for their family.

"Kirti," her father said. "you know we may have to sell you so we can have enough to feed the family. You understand that don't you?"

"Yes, Father, I understand." Kirti said softy.

Kirti knew what her father was talking about. This happens to families there. A daughter is sold to a home where she becomes a servant to the people. The people may pay a little to her family to help them get by, depending on the agreement that is made. But she has also heard of a girl who was sold and what happened to her was very bad.

Marrish did not want to do this to his daughter. He talked with some neighbors and got some vegetable seeds and gave them to Kirti.

"Here, my daughter," Marrish said. "If you can plant these and then sell some vegetables when we go to the market, then our family may do well enough to stay together."

"Thank you, Father!" Kirti said happily. "I will grow some vegetables and we will do good."

Kirti walked to the other farms in her area to learn how to grow the vegetables. When the time came, she planted them. Every day she would go out and talk to her garden about how big it was getting and how much it was producing. She has to work her garden in between the times she worked in the fields helping to tend and gather the wheat, barley, and maize with the rest of her family. They have to keep the weeds out of the fields by pulling them up. Sometimes, they have to carry water to some of the plants that don't get enough rain. They have large curved knives to cut the wheat and barley when it is time to harvest it. It is hard work. They pull the maize off the stalks when it is ready and put it in large wagons owned by the land owner. Then they have to cut down the stalks and pile them on other wagons for it to be used as animal feed.

The goats have become the only friends Kirti has. She talks to them. They raise the goats for milk and meat and also to pull the cart that carries whatever they have to the market. Scraps from the crops raised by the land owner are used to feed them.

"Jewel," Kirti said to the goat, " I don't want to live this life forever. It is hard work just trying to get enough to eat. Jewel, please find and tell the god of my future to come and help me."

Jewel just looked at her.

Her family went to New Delhi once to buy clothes, but it was very far from where they live out in the country. There she saw large buildings, shops, houses, and lots of people coming and going. It was a different world from where she lives. Since then she has often wondered what would happen to her when she becomes a grown-up. In a few years, her father would be finding a husband for her. She did not want to live her life like her parents.

"There is a big world out there I do not know Jewel." Kirti said. "Send the god to help me have a choice in my life. I do not want to marry a farmer and stay here. Please, someone, help me."

Kirti and her brothers went to school for a while. She learned to read and write and had some other basic classes. Her father and mother could not read or write, so her parents believe their children are very fortunate to have had the opportunity to learn things. From what little she learned about other areas of the world, Kirti longed to see other places and do other things with her life than work in the fields.

Late in the day when Kirti had her chores done, she would go out from her house and sit on a rock and talk out loud to Jewel. She could say whatever she felt because no one is there to hear her words.

"Someday, I will go to a big school somewhere and learn how to do a job in the city." Kirti said. "I will work and see places I have never seen before. I will marry a man in the city and we will have a house there. I will not have to work in the fields anymore. I will be very happy!"

Kirti's family are Hindu. They do believe in gods, but do not practice their beliefs like some other families do. Sometimes she would finish her work in the field and in her garden and she would go away to her rock and pretend she was somewhere else having a different life.

"Please, god, send someone to help me get away from here." Kirti would often say words like these to Jewel. Or "I wish I was away from here and living somewhere else where I can have a different life and be happy."

Kirti did not talk to her mother about her dreams, and especially she did not tell her father because it would make him feel bad about the life he has provided for them. One day as Kirti looked out over the land while sitting on her rock, she saw in the distance a faint figure walking towards her. It looked like a glowing white figure with large wings, but as it got nearer the wings disappeared and the figure became a young farmer.

He had on brown boots, tan baggy pants and a green checked shirt. His hair was straight, black and cut short. His dark brown eyes looked at her and sparkled.

He smiled and said, "Hello Kirti. I am Atul. I have been sent to make things happen in answer to your pleas. Just follow along with me and I will open doors that will cause your life to change."

"You came out of that light!" Kirti said. "How did you do that? Where did you come from?"

"Someday you will understand." Atul told her. "I am your friend. I have to get some things lined up for you. I will be back in a few days and I will tell you more then. I have to get to the Asian Mission in the city and work things out there." Atul walked back in the direction he came till he was out of sight.

Kirti and her father had to go to the nearest town to sell vegetables. Marrish and Ria Adetta do not have a car to use for travel. Her dad strapped the goat to the cart and loaded it with all it could carry. The market was several miles away and would take them hours to walk there. They started that day before daylight.

They set up their vegetables at the market with the others. Kirti stayed to sell them there while her father took some to sell to the surrounding neighborhoods. As Kirti waited for someone to come and buy her vegetables, a man and woman walked up and spoke to her. Standing behind the woman was Atul looking at her and smiling.

"Talk to these people," Atul said to her. "They can do a lot to help you."

The man and woman began to talk to Kirti.

"Hello," the woman said to Kirti. "My name is Mrs. Howard. I work with Asia Missions School. How old are you?"

"I am eleven." Kirti answered.

"Have you gone to school?" Mrs. Howard asked.

"I went some when I was younger, but cannot go anymore. In my village, we get to learn the basics, but then we have to work and help our family make a living. That is why I am here today, to sell vegetables so we could buy things my family needs." Kirti explained.

"This is Mr. Sartain," Mrs. Howard said. "Mr. Sartain and I are visiting this area to do an outreach for Asia Missions. We do have a couple of spaces in the school that are open and we are looking for new students to work with. Do you think you would be interested?"

Kirti looked at Atul, who was still standing a ways behind Mrs. Howard. He was smiling at her and nodding his head.

"I don't think my parents can afford for me to go to your school." Kirti said as she hung her head.

It's not that kind of school." Mr Sartain said as he smiled down at her. "You can live at this school, have your own bed, plenty to eat, and learn things from having a higher education. The children there get sponsors from all over the world that pays for their school, food and their other needs while they are there. The boys and girls selected are from different areas all over India. They are from poor families and they could not go to school without Asia Missions. From this school, the children could go on to a trade school or a community college in a city where they can learn a skill that would help them get a good job."

Kirti was excited. Atul smiled at her and nodded his head. "Please talk to my father to see if I can go!" Kirti said. "

"We will come to see your father and mother in two weeks," Mrs. Howard told Kirti. "Please talk to him about this before we come."

"I will!" Kirti said with excitement.

When her father returned and the vegetables were all sold, Kirti and her father bought the supplies they needed and began the walk back home. Kirti talked excitedly to her father about all Mrs. Howard had said about the Asia Missions School. Then she told her father her dreams for a different life.

They got home and went right to bed because it was dark and they were tired. Kirti was up the next morning telling her mother about Asia Missions School. Her mother listened to her and saw Kirti's excitement about the school. Later, Ria walked around her house and looked out over the land and field where they lived and worked. She did wish a better life for her daughter, but she did not know how Marrish would feel about their daughter leaving them. They would have to talk about it. Marrish talked to Ria as she prepared their evening meal.

"Kirti really wants to go to this school," Ria told Marrish.

"I see that, but we really need her help here." Marrish said.

"If Kirti had not worked so hard on that garden, you would have sold her so we could get by and she would not be here anyway." Ria said sadly. "I know we will not get money for her, but maybe Raj can work her garden and make up for the loss."

"But we will not know what will happen to her there." Marrish replied.

"She will be more safe and happy there than if she had been sold. Kirti may never come back to work here, but isn't that what she wants?" Ria reasoned.

Later, Kirti is sitting on her rock talking to Jewel when Atul came walking up behind her.

"Atul!" Kirti said. "Thank you. What will happen if my father does not let me go?"

"We have a way of communicating God's will to people." Atul said with a smile. "Do not worry, it will all work out."

"Who are you, Atul?" Kirti asked.

"I am your angel, assigned to you by God." Atul explained. " We angels have assignments from God to carry out HIs will. When you asked for help, you asked for God to help you. So, here I am. I will always be with you, but you will not always be able to see me and talk to me as you are now. As your life changes, remember, it is Jehovah that has come to change your life. Jehovah just wants you to believe in Him from now on."

"I will." Kirti said, even though she was not sure if everything was really real or just a dream.

"Just believe things will be different for you and that you will be happy with the decisions you make." said Atul. "That is all God requires, and be thankful for what He does for you. At the Asia Missions School you will learn more about God."

Kirti was just a little fearful over what was happening because she did not know what to expect. But more than that, she was excited because her life was going to change.

 Marrish was still undecided. He wanted Kirti to be happy, but he did not know if these people could be trusted with his daughter. He went back and forth on her going and not going. That night, Atul appeared to Marrish in a dream. In the dream, Atul wore a knee-length white robe, sandals, a gold sash and had wings.

"It will be good for Kirti to go to the school." Atul said to Marrish in the dream.

"Who are you?" asked Marrish.

"I am Kirti's angel," said Atul. "Kirti spoke many times wishing for an opportunity for a different life. She will be taken care of at Asia Missions and do well there. There is a plan for Kirti's life to help other girls in your country when she is older. This school will prepare Kirti for that, and she will be very happy in doing this."

"I am worried about the rest of my family too," Marrish said to Atul.

"You will always have enough. It is in God's plan ." Atul said.

"Which god is helping my Kirti?" Marrish asked.

"It is the one true God, that loves everyone the same." Atul answered. "If you ask, more information will be given to you at a later time."

"Will you always look after her?" Marrish asked.

"Yes," answered Atul. "I will always be with her while she is here on earth. I will help guide her in the direction that is best for her. Do not worry about Kirti, she will be in God's hands."

Marrish woke up with that thought on his mind. The angel will be with his daughter all the time. He had a lot of unanswered questions about this angel and his God, but there was something about this that gave him great peace.

The next morning Marrish told Kirti about his dream. Kirti told her father about seeing Atul several times and what he looked like to her.

A couple of days later, Mr. Sartain and Mrs. Howard from Asia Missions came to their house. They drove up in an old station wagon. Mr. Sartain gave them information about the school. He explained to them about getting Kirti a sponsor and how everything at the school worked. Mr. Sartain showed Kirti and her parents pictures of the school and they liked what they saw.

"We will let Kirti go to your school." Marrish told them. Ria was happy that Marrish was letting Kirti go.

Mrs. Howard told them when she and Mr. Sartain would come and pick up Kirti and take her to the school.

"Can we come and visit Kirti?" her father asked Mr. Sartain.

"Yes, there will be times when you can come to visit her. We will bring information about the school to you when we come for her. Kirti will like it there, and she will be safe." Mr. Sartain replied.

Marrish knew that Raj or Davis could read the information to him. Something inside of him told him this was the right thing to do. A feeling of pride for Kirti was developing within him. It was something he did not expect to feel for his daughter.

They left and the Adetta's went back to work. Later that day, Kirti ran to her rock and called out for Atul.

He came walking up behind her saying, "Everything will be alright Kirti. At the school you will have your own bed, a place for your things, good food, and you will learn many things."

"I am so happy about going to school! Thank you, Atul, for this opportunity!" Kirti exclaimed.

"You will meet other girls like yourself and other people," Atul said. "You can tell people about all of this if you wish. Learn as much as you can about God, and do well in your studies. If you set goals for yourself, you can accomplish them. Your future is all up to you."

"Will you be with me at the school?" Kirti asked.

"You may not see me for a while," said Atul. "But if you need me, I will be near. You can talk to God, as you did on the rock, anytime and anyplace. He always hears you. Do not be afraid, you are not alone."

"Bye Atul!" Kirti said as he walked away.

Atul turned and waved at her.

A few days later, Mr. Sartain and Mrs. Howard came and took Kirti to the school. When they arrived at the school and as Kirti got out of the car, she looked out over the school and smiled. In her mind she could see Atul smiling at her. Kirti saw two girls about her age and walked over to them.

"Hello, my name is Kirti. What is your name?" Kirti said to them. The girls told her their names and together they walked towards the building to see Kirti's room.